THE HUNTER AND THE EBONY TREE

Written and illustrated by

Nelda LaTeef

Moon Mountain
PUBLISHING

North Kingstown, Rhode Island

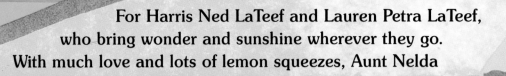

For Harris Ned LaTeef and Lauren Petra LaTeef,
who bring wonder and sunshine wherever they go.
With much love and lots of lemon squeezes, Aunt Nelda

*With special thanks, for their love and support,
to Mom, Dad, Noel, Nora, Ned and Sage.—NL*

Text and Illustrations Copyright © 2002 Nelda LaTeef

First edition.

Library of Congress Cataloging-in-Publication Data

LaTeef, Nelda, 1958-
  The hunter and the ebony tree / written and illustrated
by Nelda LaTeef.
     p. cm.
Summary: A hunter asks his friends to help him
win the hand of a beautiful girl who seeks a
husband who is special, but whose father has set
a near-impossible task to ensure that she will marry
a strong man.
  ISBN 0-9677929-9-1 (hardcover : alk. paper)
[1. Zarma (African people)—Folklore. 2. Folklore—
Africa, West. 3. Marriage—Folklore.] I. Title.
  PZ8.1.L334 Hu 2002
  [398.2]—dc21
                              2002002461

The illustrations are done in acrylic and
collage on art board. Several of the
fabric patterns are used with
the kind permission
of S. Harris.

Moon Mountain Publishing
80 Peachtree Road
North Kingstown, RI 02852
www.moonmountainpub.com

Printed in South Korea

10 9 8 7 6 5 4 3 2 1

A tall ebony tree stood in the center of the village of Tombakonda. The tree was very old and its trunk was hard and impenetrable. No arrow had ever pierced the bark.

In this same village lived a girl who was much admired for her beauty. Every day, men from all parts of the land came to ask her father for her hand in marriage.

With so many proposals, the girl's father pondered how to choose the right husband for his daughter. He believed that her extraordinary beauty would require a man of great strength to protect her.

His daughter, who was known to be as wise as she was beautiful, respectfully listened as he shared his concerns with her. When he was done speaking, she observed, "A husband must have certain qualities besides mere strength, if a marriage is to be happy and prosperous."

Seeing her father still weighed down by doubt and uncertainty, the girl offered: "Father, I have an idea. Let it be known that I will marry the man whose arrow can penetrate the trunk of the ebony tree."

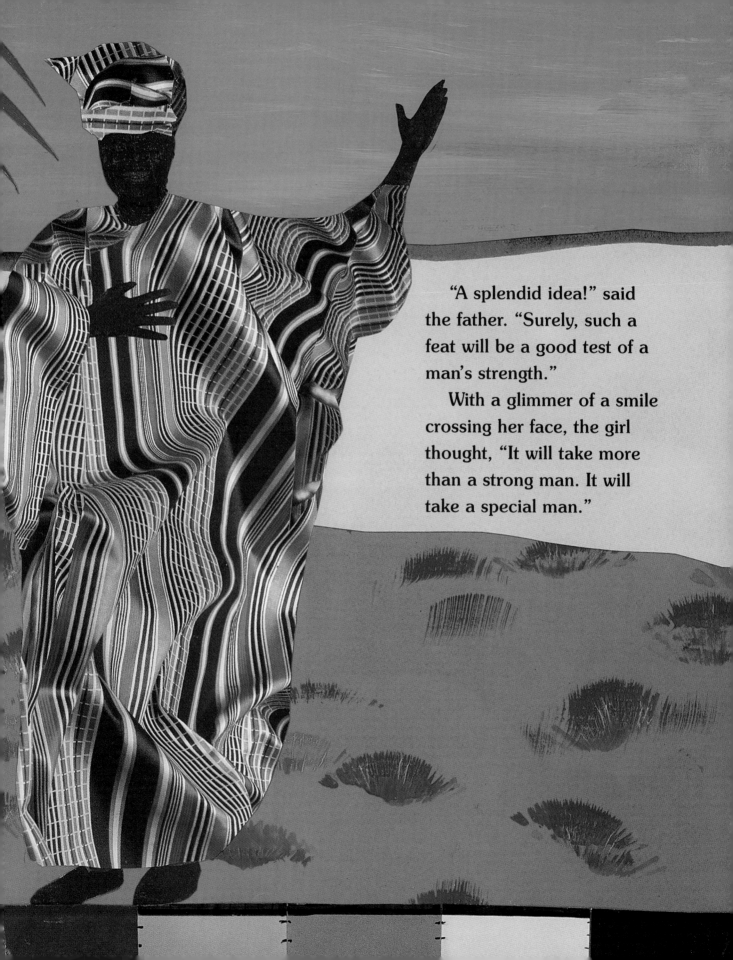

"A splendid idea!" said the father. "Surely, such a feat will be a good test of a man's strength."

With a glimmer of a smile crossing her face, the girl thought, "It will take more than a strong man. It will take a special man."

Word of the contest quickly spread.

From far and near, scores of suitors came to test their prowess. They brought bows with them of every weight and size, yet every attempt met with failure. Soon the ground around the ebony tree was littered with broken arrows, but this did not discourage their ardor, and as quickly as disappointed suitors left, hopeful new ones appeared.

One day, a handsome young hunter who was passing through Tombakonda stopped at the village well to quench his thirst. There, drawing water, was the girl.

With a shy smile, she offered him a drink from her jug. She had never done that for a stranger before. The hunter gazed into her eyes as he drank the cold water. When he finished drinking, he knew his search for a bride had come to an end.

As soon as the girl left, the hunter said to a villager standing nearby, "I am going to marry that girl! Where can I find her father?"

The villager laughed and pointed to the ebony tree. "My good fellow, you don't have to ask her father. All you have to do is shoot an arrow into that tree. Let me caution you, though. Many men far bigger and stronger than you have failed in the attempt."

The hunter went up to the ebony tree to study it. He rapped and tapped the trunk. "I cannot penetrate this thick bark with an arrow," he thought, "but with help from my friends, everything is possible." There and then he came up with a plan.

He set out in search of his friend the woodpecker. The hunter knew he could count on the woodpecker, for years earlier he had saved him from the deadly clutches of a falcon.

Hearing the distinct sound of drilling above his head, he spied his friend's red-crested head bobbing back and forth.

"Woodpecker," he hailed, "I have come to seek a favor. I need your help."

The woodpecker flew to a lower branch to hear his friend's request. When the hunter finished speaking, the woodpecker agreed to accompany him back to the village of Tombakonda.

As the village slept, and by the light of a brilliant full moon, the woodpecker drilled a hole deep into the ebony tree.

"Thank you, my friend!" the hunter called after him, as the woodpecker dipped his golden-splashed wings in the moonlit sky and flew a straight course back to his favorite tree.

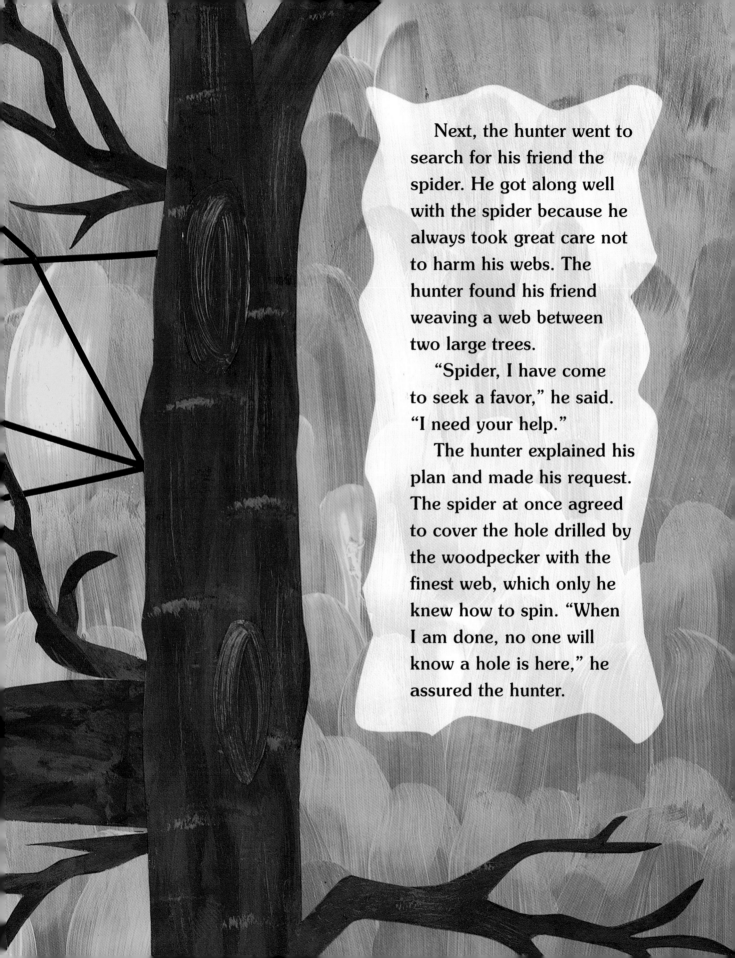

Next, the hunter went to search for his friend the spider. He got along well with the spider because he always took great care not to harm his webs. The hunter found his friend weaving a web between two large trees.

"Spider, I have come to seek a favor," he said. "I need your help."

The hunter explained his plan and made his request. The spider at once agreed to cover the hole drilled by the woodpecker with the finest web, which only he knew how to spin. "When I am done, no one will know a hole is here," he assured the hunter.

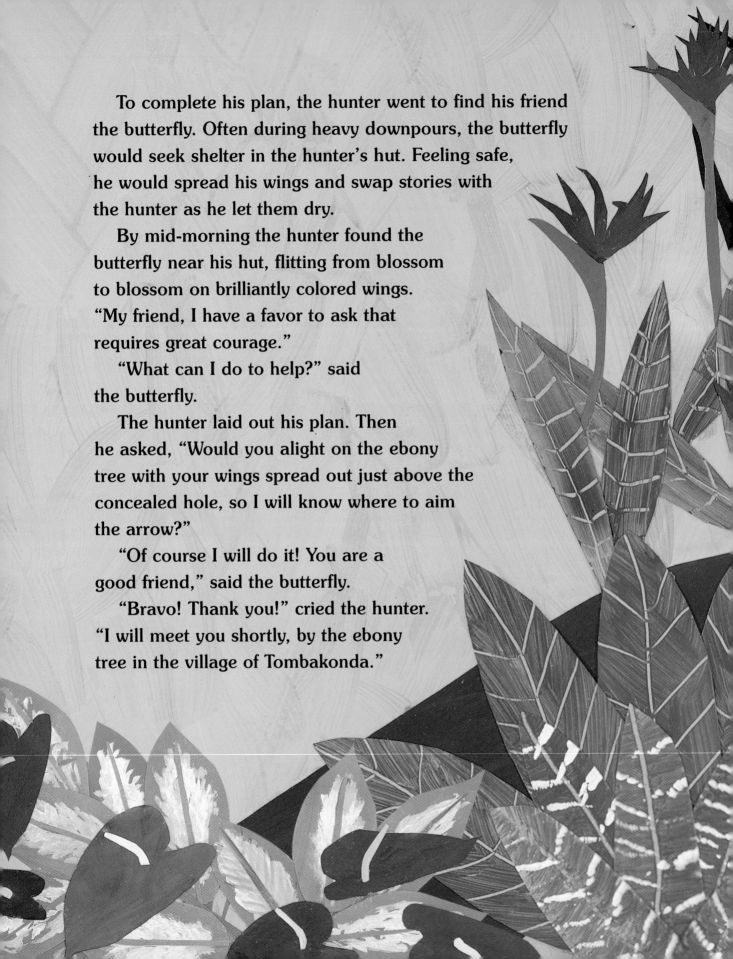

To complete his plan, the hunter went to find his friend the butterfly. Often during heavy downpours, the butterfly would seek shelter in the hunter's hut. Feeling safe, he would spread his wings and swap stories with the hunter as he let them dry.

By mid-morning the hunter found the butterfly near his hut, flitting from blossom to blossom on brilliantly colored wings. "My friend, I have a favor to ask that requires great courage."

"What can I do to help?" said the butterfly.

The hunter laid out his plan. Then he asked, "Would you alight on the ebony tree with your wings spread out just above the concealed hole, so I will know where to aim the arrow?"

"Of course I will do it! You are a good friend," said the butterfly.

"Bravo! Thank you!" cried the hunter. "I will meet you shortly, by the ebony tree in the village of Tombakonda."

The hunter went to his hut and soon came out with a large bow strapped across his broad chest and a quiver of arrows slung over his shoulder.

When he arrived at the village, clusters of villagers began to gather to witness his attempt. The girl and her father were there too.

The hunter walked twenty paces from the tree. With practiced ease, he inserted an arrow in his large bow. Then he pulled it as far back as it would bend, and aimed for a spot just below the butterfly's brilliantly colored wings.

The arrow whistled through the air and with a loud *thunk* sank deep into the ebony tree. The villagers gasped in astonishment and they began to chant: "The hunter has done it! The hunter has done it! He has pierced the ebony tree."

As the girl smiled contentedly, her father threw his hands up in the air and joyfully cried out for all to hear: "At last, my daughter has a husband who is worthy of her!"

Amidst much celebration, as the woodpecker, the spider, and the butterfly looked on, the hunter smiled and said to his beautiful bride, "My dear, with loyal friends and a good plan, everything is possible!"

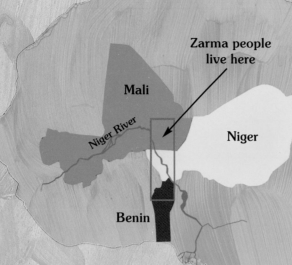

Zarma people live here

Mali

Niger River

Niger

Benin

AUTHOR'S NOTE

The Hunter and The Ebony Tree is derived from a story I heard while living in West Africa, in the Republic of Niger. The story was told by an old Zarma storyteller, or *griot* as she was called. I recorded the story on tape, and a friend later translated it for me from Zarma into French.

In the Republic of Niger, the Zarma people represent one quarter of the population and play a significant role in governing the country. The Zarma live in the western part of Niger, along the Niger River, and in the adjacent countries of Mali and Benin. They were once known as fierce warriors. Today many of them are farmers, growing millet, sorghum, corn, and peanuts in the arid lands of the Sahel, where the temperature soars above 110°F (43°C) most of the year.

The Zarma people are part of a larger West African ethnic group known as the Songhai, and their language, Zarma, is a Songhai dialect. Less than one-tenth of the Zarma are literate, and that is why the *griots*, or "guardians of old words," play an important role in the culture. The Zarma have a wise saying: "One who hears something good must repeat it."

N.L.